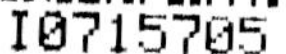

BREATHLESS

MARC JOHNSON

A SINGULARITY RISING NOVEL

A SINGULARITY RISING NOVEL

BREATHLESS

MARC JOHNSON

BREATHLESS
A Singularity Rising novel
Copyright © 2024 by Marc Johnson

All rights reserved.

No part of this publication may be reproduced, distributed, or transmitted in any form or by any means, including photocopying, recording, or other electronic or mechanical methods, without the prior written permission of the publisher, except as permitted by U.S. copyright law. For permission requests, contact marcjohnson@marcanthonyjohnson.com

The story, all names, characters, and incidents portrayed in this production are fictitious. No identification with actual persons (living or deceased), places, buildings, and products is intended or should be inferred.

Contents

CHAPTER 1

The night air was crisp, not sharp or biting. A light jacket or sweater would have been nice, but he wouldn't freeze to death without one. It was almost eleven p.m. on a Wednesday, and the streets were quiet. But in the city, there was always someone taking a late night walk, even in a fancy neighborhood like this.

A well-dressed white woman walked toward him on the wide sidewalk. Floyd smiled and said, "It's a nice night, isn't it, ma'am?"

She clutched her purse and pursed her lips, watching a car pass. He could tell she was thinking about crossing the street to avoid walking past him. She did end up crossing the street, ignoring Floyd as she did so.

Floyd had become numb to the casual racism. Yet a small voice in his head thought it may have been because of the way he was dressed. He was a hulking bald Black man in a black hoodie, with an empty black duffel bag slung over his shoulder. In a perfect world, his clothes should have nothing to do with it. But if anything went wrong, the woman, and anyone else who might have seen him, would have a hard time identifying anything specific about his face. He would be just another so-called thug.

Being in this part of the city always made him uncomfortable. And it had nothing to do with the long train ride or what he had planned.

The bank sat in the middle of the block, bright lights shining on its imposing stone blocks. The cold eye of its eagle mascot shone, watchful of any trespassers. The metal gates and thick glass were an impenetrable shield.

But not for Floyd.

He wasn't going through the front. Anyone could pass by in a car and see or record him. Floyd slipped through the alley to the back entrance, pulling the hoodie up over his head. He put on gloves to complete the costume. The doors in the alley were thicker, but there were fewer cameras and the lights were dimmer.

He held his breath and pushed on the door. The reinforced metal buckled and crumpled. Floyd could have broken and torn off the door completely. Instead, he squeezed through the crack in the solid metal door.

Because of Floyd's brute force, he knew the alarm had been tripped. He ran straight to the vault. Juan had cased the bank for the last couple of weeks. Floyd held his breath again and punched the steel door, making a large dent in the center. He punched again using more force and the door gave way, hanging on its hinges.

The hard part was stuffing the money into the duffel bag. He was strong, not quick, and the thick gloves he wore didn't make things any easier. The excitement always made his heart beat faster and sweat drip down his bald head.

Floyd counted the passing seconds silently, as he always did, allowing himself to get to precisely one eighty. He never got all the money, but better to get some and get away than get caught. Floyd zipped up the bag, making sure no money stuck out, and sprinted out of the bank.

The sounds of sirens rung in his ears. He cursed. He had either been too slow or the white woman called the cops before he had even gotten to the bank. They were getting close. He had maybe two minutes at best. There was a reason they decided to rob banks in white neighborhoods. Aside from being the right thing to do, the cops were a little slower to respond than in Black neighborhoods, and there were never any security patrols. After all, who would be foolish enough to rob them?

He grinned. *Floyd Taylor, that's who.*

As he ran by a large trash bin, Frank tossed in the duffel and reached into one of the holes on the side to pull out a black garbage bag. As he hurried down the alleyway, he dug into the bag, pulling out a clean white button-down. He frowned at the thick creases. *Juan should have known better than to give me a wrinkled shirt.*

Floyd stuffed his hoodie into the bag and threw it to the side of the alley. He tucked his shirt into his jeans and held his head high as the sirens reached his location. Police cars raced by while patrolmen on foot headed in his direction.

The cops stopped when they saw Floyd. He looked directly at them and said, "Is there a problem, officers?"

The pair eyed him, their fingers dangling on their guns. "What are you doing here?" the older one said.

Floyd kept his breathing and heart rate normal. He had dealt with this dozens of times. It wasn't his nervousness that bothered him. It was his anger. He needed to keep that in check.

He failed. "I got off work late. Is it a crime for a Black man to walk at night?"

The portly older cop stepped forward. "Listen, boy—"

The scrawny younger cop grabbed his partner. "Come on, Al. He didn't do it. Boy is too pretty. And do you see a black hoodie anywhere? We gotta go."

Al grunted and took off after his partner.

Floyd unclenched his fist. *Stupid.* He almost let his anger get the best of him. After all these centuries, they still think of his people as guilty. Floyd couldn't help but smile. This time they were right.

Before any more cops could stop him and run his ID, Floyd disappeared into the city, leaving his money behind.

CHAPTER 2

Dragging his feet and yawning, Floyd reached Juan's apartment. Robbing banks was a tiring pastime. At least he would be able to get a few hours of sleep and take a hot shower before he needed to change into his work overalls. Although there was a dark stain on them that he hadn't been able to get out that still bothered him.

Floyd leaned against Juan's door and knocked, the raised number eleven pressing into his forehead. The door opened and Floyd nearly fell in.

"Whoa, amigo," Juan said. "There's the man of the hour. Come in, come in! I got breakfast for you."

Juan went into the kitchen. Floyd shut the door and sat down on the couch. He tried to eat healthily but Juan's choice of food was always something greasy.

"Is that a breakfast sandwich?" Floyd asked, his nose sniffing.

"You know it. With chorizo. And a fresh coffee."

"Thanks."

Floyd took a large bite of the delicious sandwich. He let out a moan.

"Sorry there's no room on the table." Juan's eyes were bright. He was wide awake even though he also had been up all night.

Floyd's eyes went to the stacks and stacks of money on the table. The duffel bag he had used was empty on the floor.

"How much?" Floyd asked.

"A little over a hundred grand." Juan whistled. "That was quite a score."

Floyd nodded. "Good. We haven't had a score like that in a while."

"The gringos have all the money." Juan patted his friend on the shoulder. "Since we have such a big score, how about twenty percent instead of fifteen?"

Floyd took a sip of his black coffee. "You know this money isn't for me."

"I know, Robin Hood. I know." Juan shrugged and took a bite of his sandwich. "Could always go after the banks in our own neighborhoods. Get a lot more money."

He sighed. They had had this discussion many times before. But Floyd wasn't about to rob his own people, no matter how much more difficult it was. The police would be swarming his neighborhoods, making lives more difficult than they already did. Floyd allowed himself a little smile. He did feel like Robin Hood, and this was his way of sticking it to the man.

"You know I'm not going to."

"You're the boss," Juan said, putting his hands up. "Just a thought. Far less risk and more money."

"Risk for yourself, maybe, but not for the people here."

"You're the one with the powers. I'm just the one who scouts the bank and retrieves the money."

Juan turned away, but Floyd knew what he meant. One time the money went missing before the police left the scene and Juan could grab the bag. Floyd hoped whoever found it got to enjoy themselves and, with any luck, stayed off the streets. Even though it didn't bother Floyd too much, Juan wouldn't stop pestering him about it for weeks afterward.

"You sure I can't get a little more? It was a long way to get there and back..."

Floyd rubbed his temples. He was hoping this wouldn't come up, but it seemed to after every job.

"Sorry, man," Floyd said, as he always did. "Can't do it. At least right now. There's just so much I need to do with the money."

Juan grabbed Floyd's empty plate. "I get it."

"You sure?"

Juan smiled. "Yeah, man. We good. Just thought I'd ask. You know me. Always trying to make an extra buck."

Floyd returned his smile and checked his watch. It was time to go. He wiped his mouth and gulped the rest of his coffee. A gigantic toolbox sat next to the table. Floyd stuffed the money in the bottom before putting his tools on top.

He grunted, lifting it. "Money is far heavier when you have to carry it by hand rather than over your shoulder."

"You could take your tools out."

"They provide cover, and I need them."

"Why not use your powers?" Juan asked.

"I do, but I can't hold my breath forever. I gotta go, but let me know what bank you want to hit up next."

Juan stroked his chin. "I have a few ideas, but we should lay low. Heat is getting real thick in the air, and it's not gonna be good for Blacks in hoodies."

Floyd sighed. "When is it ever?"

He left Juan's apartment and trudged to the high-rise apartment building at the end of the block. He used his powers to carry the heavy box, but every time he had to take a breath, the pain ran down his arm and into the lower back.

When Floyd got to the apartment building, he stopped and set the toolbox down. He checked his phone, seeing the messages Mr. Patterson had sent: backed-up toilet in apartment 33, dripping faucet in apartment 60, no hot water in apartment 12, mold in apartment 80. The list went on and on. Most would have to wait. He had far more important things to do today.

The first apartment Floyd went to was Mr. Florence. He heard the loud TV from the end of the hall. It took several tries, but eventually Mr. Florence answered the door.

"WHAT?" he yelled. "You don't need to knock so loud. Floyd, it's you. Didn't think you'd be here. Nothing here needs fixing, except for me, that is."

"I'm not here for that," Floyd said. "I'm here for...something else." He winked, but Mr. Florence didn't understand.

"What? Speak up, boy! I can't hear you."

"I said, I'm here for something else!"

"Huh?"

It was useless. Floyd reached into his toolbox and pulled out a brick of cash. For once, Mr. Florence was speechless.

Tears welled in Mr. Florence's eyes. "My hip...Floyd, I can't take this. Where did you get it?"

"Don't worry about it, Mr. Florence. Just get that hip replacement you've been talking about."

At first, Floyd wasn't sure if Mr. Florence heard him over the blaring game show, but finally Mr. Florence smiled and said, "Thank you."

The next apartment would be easier than Mr. Florence's. They had their own problems, but at least there wouldn't be any yelling. The door opened before he finished knocking. A large smile greeted him.

"Morning, Floyd," she said.

"Morning, Shanice."

Her eyebrows rose. "You always impress me with your punctuality."

Floyd turned his head, the heat rising in his cheeks.

Shanice grabbed him by the arms, reeling him inside.

"I wish you came by more often, Floyd," Shanice said.

"I'm a busy man." Although on those cold, lonely nights, he wished differently.

"Uh-huh."

Floyd put the heavy toolbox down and sat on the couch. He moved his tools aside, digging into it while Shanice slid up against him on the couch. Water clung to Shanice's ebony skin, as did the thin robe she wore. Floyd found himself staring too long and caught himself, but not before she saw him and smiled.

He cleared his throat and handed her a stack of cash. "This is for you and James. I know his dad doesn't help and you need money for school supplies, clothes, and everything."

Shanice leaned in closer but didn't take the money. She whispered into his ear, "You don't have to only come by and drop off money. I'd prefer it if you didn't."

Floyd started to lean closer when a loud thumping noise approached.

"Floyd!"

"Hey James." Floyd closed his toolbox.

Shanice slid her hand across Floyd's lap as she reached for the money, then tightened her robe as James jumped between them on the couch.

"Mom said you were coming by today. She said she needed fixing."

"Oh, did she?" Floyd said, grinning. "How's the fifth grade?"

"Boring, just trying to make it to the sixth."

Floyd nodded. "I'm sure you will. Feel like sixth grade is when you finally become a man."

"Really?" James asked.

"Yup. That was the best time of my life. We would play ball in the streets and I started to notice girls around then too. Got into some trouble because of that."

"You did?" Shanice asked.

Floyd glanced at his watch. "I should go. I have more work to do."

"But you just got here," James said, pouting. Shanice made the same face, but Floyd pretended not to notice.

"I know, little man." Floyd ruffled James's hair. "But you got to finish getting ready for school, and your mom for work. I'll be back later today. Promise."

James smiled, but there was a hint of sadness in his eyes.

"Let me walk you to the door," Shanice said. She grabbed Floyd's free arm and entwined it with hers. At the door, she reached up on her toes and kissed Floyd on the cheek. "Thanks for stopping by. I hope you'll keep your promise and come by later tonight. If not for me, then for him."

Floyd looked back toward James's room. He had been raised by a single mother too, and knew the value of a father's promise, and the pain when it wasn't fulfilled.

"I will." He meant it. Not just to see James, but because he ached to see Shanice.

When Floyd walked through the door, Shanice slapped him on the ass. "Good. See you tonight."

Out of the long list Mr. Patterson gave Floyd, he only finished two small things. The rest of the day was spent giving people money. There was Mrs. Wong on the fifth floor who needed cancer treatments, the young couple in the corner apartment whose dog just died but they were still paying off the vet bills, a single mom who needed her car repaired to get to work, and a young college student drowning in debt.

While Floyd initially felt good helping people by giving them money, it was fleeting. There were so many people just one paycheck or hospital bill from being evicted. *We're all closer to being homeless than being rich.* The whole system needed to be taken down, but Floyd was just one man.

Floyd walked the halls and yawned. It had been a long day. The bottom layer of the toolbox was almost empty. But what wore him out were all the sad stories, and seeing the people's faces light up when he gave them the money.

Floyd put a hand to his belly. There was also a lot of food pushed on him by grateful neighbors.

As Floyd turned the corner, he nearly ran over an older man in the hallway. With his free hand, Floyd steadied him before he toppled.

The man scowled, pushing his large plastic glasses up onto the ridge of his nose. "Watch where you're going!" He tucked his overly large button-up shirt back into the pants.

"Sorry, Mr. Patterson."

"Floyd. Hmmm...thought it was you. Have you finished apartment sixty?"

Floyd frowned. "Apartment sixty?"

Mr. Patterson nodded. "Yes, there's a new tenant complaining about a broken garbage disposal."

"That's impossible. That apartment was renovated and newly painted after Mrs. Frisby passed."

The landlord scrunched his face. "I remember. I also remember what a hoarder that woman was. Mice and roaches everywhere. Had to pay to get the entire building pest control for a year."

He acts like he was the one who had to clean up the mess.

"Just go and see what he wants," Mr. Patterson said.

"Yes, sir."

As Floyd walked down the hallway, he heard Mr. Patterson mutter to himself, "Kids today. Always whining over every little thing in their apartment. I'm too old for this."

Floyd smiled. Mr. Patterson may have been a grumbling old man, but he was fair. He paid well, and he never talked down to Floyd or micromanaged. He was also lenient when people were late with their rent. But not too lenient.

Apartment sixty was newly renovated with one of the highest rents. Floyd worked on that unit for months. There should be no issues with it.

Floyd knocked on the apartment door, which almost immediately opened to reveal a man in his late twenties.

The man grinned at Floyd and stuck out his hand. "You must be Floyd. I'm Samar. Nice to meet you."

Samar's dark curly hair hung down to his shoulders, and his cargo pants and T-shirt were loose around his body. He moved aside. "Come in, come in."

"What seems to be the problem?" Floyd asked. "I just ran into Mr. Patterson and he said you're having issues with the garbage disposal." He glanced around the apartment. Stacked boxes were everywhere and empty containers of takeout noodles covered the counters. "I find that hard to believe."

Samar grinned. "You got me there. I wanted to see you, and figured this would be the fastest way."

Floyd let out a deep breath, setting down his tool-box. "Oh."

"I heard you're a guy who knows how to get things."

Floyd shrugged, praying that this wasn't going to be the same conversation he'd had dozens of times before.

"I can get a few things," Floyd said. "Things like new tile, carpet, curtain rods, cabinets, good wood, and solid piping. If you need something for your apartment or your family's house, I can help out with that."

Samar scratched his head. "That's not what I meant at all." He looked down at the floor before looking up and meeting Floyd's eyes. "I heard you can get people money. I need money. Not too much, just enough."

Floyd looked around the bare studio apartment. No pictures on the walls, no video game console, no couch. Samar had a mattress but no bed frame.

Maybe Samar did need money. But how did he afford the apartment?

"I got debt man," Samar said. "School debt, credit card debt, gambling debt. All I need is a little help to get out from under it. I just need a little cash to buy me some time."

Floyd rubbed the bridge of his nose. He'd heard stories like this before. What bothered him was how Samar knew. People talked, yes, but it took time. There were rules. And Samar was a new tenant. There was a line as long as Floyd's arm that needed his help.

Floyd sighed and picked up his toolbox. "I can't help you." He started to walk away when Samar grabbed his arm.

"Please, I'm begging you."

Floyd wished he could do something. But most of the money was gone, and the little that was left was already promised.

"Sorry, man," Floyd said. "I can't help you."

Samar pulled his hand away. "Some hero you are. I'm going to tell everyone about you. See what kind of fraud you are."

Floyd caught the desperation in his eyes. But behind it was great sadness and fear.

"You do what you have to do."

CHAPTER 3

Floyd tugged on the collar of his polo as the night breeze breathed down his neck. He'd kill for a hoodie or a jacket in this chilly air. But since he was going to rob a bank, his clothes needed to be light so he could take them off in a hurry. The weatherman said it wasn't supposed to be this cold. As usual, he was wrong. It was times like this when Floyd wished he kept his hair instead of shaving it off.

Floyd reached the alley and found the garbage bin hiding the bag of clothes. He quickly changed, eyeing the bank at the other end of the alley. He hated stuffing the clothes back in without folding them but there was never any time.

As Floyd pulled the hoodie over his head, he frowned. It had only been two weeks since the last heist. This was far too soon. Normally they took any-where from a month to three months. They never had a set amount of time. Less chance of getting caught that way. But more and more people kept asking for Floyd's help.

Floyd knew it was a bad idea, but Juan had the next job already lined up. Floyd trusted him, both with his secret and with the jobs.

It wasn't long before Floyd busted back out from the bank, the new duffel bag full of money. Not as much money as last time, but it would do.

When Floyd reached the dumpster, he dropped the bag in. His hand searched for the garbage bag but came up empty. His heart raced as he scrambled to find his clothes. He peeked in and around the dump-ster, ignoring the rank smell of trash and rats scram-bling out of his way.

"Shit," he said quietly.

Maybe if he played it cool and walked away before the cops came? Floyd shook his head. That wasn't going to work. Black people in hoodies got harassed and shot for walking down the street. The fact that the bank's alarm was shrieking wasn't going to do Floyd any favors.

Sirens blared at the end of the alley. Floyd froze. He had taken too much time looking for his clothes. *I need to leave. Now!*

Floyd ran toward the opposite end of the alley. Two police cars pulled in and blocked his path. Their doors flung open and the cops pointed their guns at Floyd.

"FREEZE!" one yelled.

He was completely surrounded.

"Put your hands up and lay down on the ground! Now!"

Floyd didn't move. The cops approached, and all he could think about was the time he was harassed by the cops for DWB—Driving While Black. He remembered being so frustrated at the time. How when he tried to calmly talk his way out of it, he couldn't. How little and inhuman the cops made him feel.

That was a long time ago. Now the police weren't in a position to do anything he didn't want them to.

Floyd held his breath. He wiggled his fingers against the palm of his hand to wipe the sweat from it. A crescendo of gunfire rang in the alleyway.

The bullets ripped through Floyd's sweatshirt and bounced off his hardened skin. The police stopped firing and stood with their mouths agape.

"What in god's name?"

Slamming his fist into the ground, Floyd sucked in a quick breath. Shockwaves rippled through the ground. The cops stumbled, light bulbs shattered, and car alarms went off.

There was no time for Floyd to think. He ran, barreling into a cop car. It smashed into the side of the building. He made it out of the alleyway, the screaming cops yelling for someone to stop him. Floyd knew this city well, and he disappeared into its embrace.

CHAPTER 4

Sirens followed Floyd through the night as he charged down the city streets. But they never seemed to get too close as he cut through back alleys and apartment buildings. *Was I really in there that long?* That would explain how his clothes got stolen. It had happened before. But the cops came way too fast. There was something off about it that bothered Floyd. He kept running over things in his head, trying to see where he or Juan had gotten sloppy.

Floyd reached Juan's apartment and pounded way too loudly on the door for the middle of the night. The sweat dripped down his bald head and his heart thumped loudly in his chest while he waited for his friend to answer the door.

As soon as Juan undid the locks, Floyd forced himself inside and quickly locked it.

"Damn, amigo," Juan said. "Heard you had a rough night. Didn't think I'd see you again. There's a lot of heat on you right now."

"No shit."

"What happened?"

Floyd pushed past his friend and headed to the kitchen. He grabbed a cup and raided the fridge for water. His parched mouth demanded sustenance. The constant running and use of his powers drained him. Floyd drank two glasses of water, then wiped the slime around his mouth.

"I'm not sure what happened," Floyd said. "The clothes were gone.""You think someone took them?"

Floyd shrugged. "I don't know. I wasn't there that long. And the cops came quicker than normal."

"I hear that. The place was swarming with cops. I wasn't even able to get the cash." Disappointment veiled Juan's face, and Floyd felt a bit guilty for letting him down.

"They're onto you, amigo," Juan said. "You know how jittery they are about rich white people getting robbed, and you just robbed two with the quickness." Juan clapped his hand on Floyd's back and whispered, "You need to lay low right now, man."

Floyd stared at his friend. "Do they have a good look at my face?"

Juan shook his head. "Nah. But they have your build and clothing. It's not gonna be safe on the streets for you or any other Blacks—especially if they gotta hoodie."

Floyd snorted. "What else is new? It's never safe for us."

"I know, but you have to be careful now. Extra careful."

"You're right," Floyd said, nodding. "I shouldn't even be here right now."

Juan smiled. "It's all good. I appreciate you thinking you could come here as your safe haven."

"I got nowhere else to go."

"You're always welcome here."

Juan was right. The streets were extremely hot. Everywhere Floyd went, he saw cops. They weren't just around banks either. They were on the street corner, in the parks, in front of churches. A week had passed since Floyd robbed the bank, but it never got any better. Police harassed normal people. There was a brief moment when Floyd felt guilty about that, but then he remembered that cops can be traced back to the Slave Patrols centuries ago. And the cops are still doing the same job centuries later. Their uniforms are different but their tactics are the same.

Floyd risked returning to his apartment to grab some clothes and a charger. Instead of staying at his apartment, he holed up in a motel for a couple of days. He told Mr. Patterson that he had a family emergency he needed to take care of. Mr. Patterson was surprisingly understanding.

For three days, Floyd barely left his room. He watched TV and searched the Internet for any news stories about him. There were crazy rumors. Rumors about a secret organization of Black men robbing banks. One said the banks were robbing themselves so they could get insurance money. Another explained that the water poisoned people and gave them powers. That one, Floyd thought might have been right.

Luckily, none of the footage they caught had a clear picture of him even with all the technology they had today. As long as he didn't wear a dark hoodie, Floyd should be fine. The local news cycle was starting to get bored of him anyway.

Floyd grabbed a light jacket and went to the corner store. He had put it off for as long as he could, but he needed fresh food not from the shady diner next to the motel. His room had a mini fridge and small stove. He wasn't the best cook, but he'd survive off milk, eggs, cheese, and tortillas if he had to.

When Floyd stepped inside the corner store, he subtly scanned for any signs of police. Cops always went to local stores—the owners knew the neighborhood and people best. He quickly grabbed the things he needed and shoved them into a basket. As he rushed around a corner, he bowled over someone half his size.

The young kid crashed into the aisle and grunted.

"Sorry about that," Floyd said, helping him up.

"It's OK. My bag took the brunt of it anyway."

"What are you doing with such a large bag? The thing is bigger than you, and almost as big as your hair." Floyd smiled and indicated the kid's gigantic afro with his eyes.

The kid grinned. "I know. But it's my turn to make a supply run."

Supply run? Odd way to say he needed food. But Floyd couldn't keep up with the way kids spoke these days.

The kid's eyes narrowed. "Do I know you? You look familiar."

A lump caught in Floyd's throat. He hoped not. There were only six people in the small store, but it only took one to get the ball rolling.

"Are you...an uncle of mine?" the kid asked.

Floyd relaxed his shoulders and let out a breath. "No, kid. I'm not."

"Oh sorry. You just look like him, and I haven't seen him in a while." The kid looked down and his eyes were heavy. "I miss him."

"What do you mean you haven't seen him?" The bell in the corner store went off, announcing another customer. Floyd turned to look back at the kid, but he was gone.

Floyd peered around the shop. The kid may have been small but with that giant bag and hair he should have been easy to spot. As more people funneled into the store, Floyd returned to his shopping. The kid must have had to return home.

He left the store and again wished he had his hoodie. The cold breeze still floated throughout the city, although winter was a few short months away.

At the end of the block, two cops stood. One, tall lengthy one who swiveled his head like a crane, and a short fat one with a coffee in his hand. Most people moved around them, but a group of teenagers coming from the basketball courts didn't swerve. They talked and laughed as they dribbled the ball between them.

The ball bounced awkwardly off the sidewalk, careening into one of the cop's legs.

"My bad," the kid said, holding his arms out for the ball.

"My bad?" the cop said, picking up the ball. "Is that any way to talk to an officer of the law? You almost knocked the coffee out of my hand."

The teenager glanced around. "Uh, no...sir. Can I get my ball back?"

The cop sauntered over with the basketball. He glared at the teenagers. "This yours?"

"Yeah."

"Not anymore." The white cop kicked the ball far down the street, toward a steep hill, and the other one smirked.

"Hey!" the teenager said. "What'd you do that for, asshole?"

The six teenagers stepped closer, loosely circling the pair. The coffee splattered on the ground as the cops drew their weapons.

"Stay back! Don't get any closer!" Sweat ran down their temples as itchy trigger fingers gripped their guns.

Floyd knew what would happen next. He had lived with it his entire life, whether it was on the Internet, the news, or in his own neighborhood. He knew he should have walked away. But he wasn't going to. He actually had the power to do something about it.

Floyd walked over to them with his hands up, still full of groceries, and held his breath. The white cop swung his loaded weapon his way. Loud noises popped in Floyd's ears before he even had a chance to speak.

The groceries splattered to the ground. The bullets ripped into the thin plastic and Floyd's clothes.

Floyd stood, unhurt, unmoving.

"Wh-what are you?" the cop asked.

Floyd stepped closer and grabbed the gun, crushing it in his hands. Anger burned in his eyes. "A Black man."

He shoved and the cop went flying ten feet in the air until he smashed into a light pole. Floyd smacked the other cop in the head as light as he could. The cop crumpled to the ground.

"You kids all right?" Floyd said, turning to the teenagers.

The one who had started the whole thing by dribbling basketball put a hand to his mouth. "Yo...you him, man! Yo, you the dude I heard about! The one who's robbing banks and giving it to the people. The Bulletproof Negro."

Floyd cocked his head. *Is that what they've been calling me?*

The teenagers began to crowd him, grabbing at his bullet filled clothes, poking his arms, bombarding him with questions.

"How'd you do that?"

"How are you alive?"

"My moms ain't gonna believe this."

For once in his life, Floyd was thankful for the sound of sirens. He didn't want to answer any questions.

"I gotta go," Floyd said.

"No problem," the one who had the basketball said. "We got your back! Good looking out!"

Floyd pushed through the gathering crowd and away from the encroaching sirens. *Where am I going to go now?* He needed a place to hide, to think. He couldn't go to Juan's. He didn't want to put his friend in danger. Nor could he turn to Shanice. She had a son to think about. He couldn't return to his motel room and he didn't have enough money to keep bouncing around. He may have been lucky before, but someone was sure to get a picture of his face now. Hiding would be impossible.

He was going to have to do something he hadn't done in a long time—return to the streets.

CHAPTER 5

It had been many years since Floyd was on the streets. He did what he had to do to help his mom out. While he was big, he never took to football nor was he ever good with words. His size was good enough for him to protect his so-called friends and collect money for them when they needed it. He never felt good beating on someone who was strung out or half his size.

There were times when he hid from both his mom and the gangs. He tried to remember those places now. There was that abandoned theater where they used to have parties. No, that place was an apartment complex now. There was the warehouse at the corner that—no, that was a Safeway now. The church still stood. It wasn't abandoned or demolished. There was a gym and shower attached to it. One of the windows of the gym could be unlocked if you slid your hand around it. He just hoped that old tree was still there and that his arms fit through the window.

In case that didn't work, Floyd needed a backup plan. And he couldn't do it on an empty stomach. The stupid cop had shot up his groceries.

Might as well grab a bite to eat first.

Floyd's stomach took him to a great hot dog place nearby. The small food joint was always crowded. There was never any seating at the two tiny tables inside. The constant line moved fast, and there were only a dozen items on the bright-colored menu. The people weren't the only ones who enjoyed this place. There was a video that went viral a couple years ago about a rat that dragged a hot dog as big as him right out the front door.

Floyd inhaled as he grabbed his order, letting the warmth of the aroma seep into his nose. He opened his mouth as wide as he could before taking a bite of the big, juicy dog. The juices, onions, and relish flowed into his mouth and down his throat. It had been far too long. A couple rose from one of the three outside tables. Just his luck. He grabbed a stool and sat down, enjoying his meal. He had just finished his dog, tempted to get another one, when someone spoke from behind him.

"I'm glad I'm not the only one who enjoys a good hot dog," the man said. "There's nothing like this where I come from. The only dogs they have are those ones made from processed meat."

Floyd froze, shifting his weight to rise. Usually he'd be annoyed by a stranger talking to him while he ate. A small man stood three feet away from him, a long ponytail falling down the back of his clean black suit. Floyd relaxed slightly. It wasn't uncommon for tourists to come here. The hole-in-the-wall was famous.

Floyd wiped his mouth with a napkin. "I've been coming here forever. You get real meat here, not that crap they serve kids."

The man nodded. "Wish there were more places like this. You got any recommendations?"

Floyd shrugged. "I mean, I like the works, but some people prefer it without toppings or there's a spicy one that's popular. Not for me though. Can't handle it."

"Oooh, spicy one sounds good. Thanks for the help...Floyd."

Floyd's back tensed.

"What do you want?" Floyd asked.

"To talk. Honest. And maybe get a hot dog." He looked back toward the entrance to the restaurant. "But if I did, I have a feeling you'd run."

Floyd allowed himself a small smile. He wasn't wrong.

"Before you decide to fight or flight, you should hear what I have to say."

Floyd looked the man up and down. He might not have been a cop, but he was something else—maybe a Fed, but even that felt wrong. Floyd thought he was more than that.

"And what is that?" Floyd asked.

"You think you're the only one with powers?"

Floyd let the man get a hot dog. Cortez, he said his name was. That's all he got out of him.

Floyd watched as Cortez ate his spicy dog. He had way too much sauerkraut on it.

"You want one?" Cortez asked in between bites. "My treat."

Floyd shook his head. He could have eaten another, but was more interested in what Cortez had to say. Floyd kept glancing around, eyeing everyone who went by, watching a few white vans as they passed.

"Don't worry," Cortez said. "I'm alone." He took the last bite of his dog. "Delicious." He slurped his drink until the cup made noises. "Fresh-squeezed. I know the hot dogs get all the rep, but the lemonade is damned good too."

Cortez stood and stretched his legs. "Let's go for a walk." He patted his stomach. "I need to work some of this off."

Floyd stared at Cortez.

"It's not a trap. So untrustworthy. Besides, you're a bulletproof Robin Hood twice my size. Trust me, I'm not armed." He lifted the flaps of his suit jacket. "Haven't earned it yet."

Floyd sighed. "Fine." It was the only way he was going to get any answers.

The pair navigated the city streets. It was a weekday and getting late, but that didn't stop the city's bustle. Cars sped by on narrow streets, bright billboards illuminated their walk, and groups of people went about their evening.

Floyd walked slightly behind Cortez. "What did you mean earlier? About how I'm not the only one?"

"You are a Singularity," Cortez said.

"A what?"

"A Singularity." He shrugged. "Something the eggheads came up with. Has to do with math, I think, but in simple terms, it means you're unique. You have powers—a gift, a curse—call it what you will."

"You said there were others," Floyd said. "How does that make me unique?"

Cortez chuckled. "You're right. Maybe rare would be a better term. These days, more and more people like yourself are being discovered."

"How long have there been...Singularities?"

Cortez paused and looked up at the night sky. "A long time. Be thankful you weren't around when you would have been burned as a witch." He resumed walking. "There's no reasoning as to why it happens or when. Sometimes it's kids, other times it's adults. When the hormonal teenagers get it, that's when trouble happens."

Floyd nodded. He could only imagine what kind of trouble he would have gotten into if he had these powers when he was younger. Floyd stopped, staring at Cortez's back and his black suit. He may not have been a cop, but he was something else—something far more dangerous.

"What's your role in this?" Floyd asked.

Cortez turned around. "Here's my favorite part. I work for an organization that tracks people like yourself."

"And imprisons them?"

Cortez shook his head and laughed. "No. We help them, train them to use their powers. It can be dangerous out on your own. You gave money to people who need it. Sure, you robbed banks. But other people have done far worse and not helped the needy." Cortez's eyes were heavy and he looked away.

Floyd stared at Cortez. There was something he wasn't telling him.

"How can I trust you?" Floyd asked.

Cortez's face grew heavy. He opened his mouth and paused. His big, wide eyes stared back at Floyd. "I was like you, alone and confused, unsure of my place in the world, but then they found me. The Agency helped me understand and control my powers. I'd probably be in jail or dead if it wasn't for them. The same path you were on before."

"What about the cops?"

Cortez waved his hand. "They wouldn't be a problem anymore. You couldn't go back to your old life, but a whole new world would open up for you."

Floyd thought about his words. It hadn't been very long, but he was getting tired of running. Running away from your problems was easier to do when you were young.

And the cops weren't his biggest issue. Ever since Floyd got his powers, he had tried to learn more about them and the things he could do. Why him? He had a feeling that whoever Cortez worked for would be able to give him some answers, but what would it cost? Something like this wouldn't come free.

"What would I have to do?" Floyd asked.

Cortez shrugged. "Whatever they say. You wouldn't start where I'm at. You'd have to work up to be in the field. You wouldn't be robbing banks anymore, I know that."

"Can I choose what I want to do with my powers within reason?"

Cortez stroked his chin. "It's not up to me."

"I know, but you know how it is."

He grinned. "I like you, Floyd. You have good taste in food and remind me of where I came from." The smile faded from his face. "You get told what to do. They say, 'jump,' you say, 'how high.' You know what

I mean? The Agency assigns you based on what they need and what they think you'd be useful at.

"This is a different world than what you're used to, but the same rules still apply. Doesn't matter whether you're a Singularity or not."

Floyd sighed and nodded. He knew exactly what Cortez meant. The game may change but the rules still stayed the same. It was going to take more than Floyd robbing banks to change things. It was going to have to be a ground swell, like those riots a few years ago when people realized how bad things were. It lasted for a moment in the grand scheme of things, but what a moment.

If Floyd joined this organization, he wasn't going to be able to make a difference. He wasn't going to be able to help people.

"I appreciate the offer," Floyd said, "but I'm gonna have to go at it my way."

Cortez shook his hand. "I respect that. I truly do."

"Thanks." Floyd took a step back, relieved that it didn't come to anything more. Cortez was far more likable than he thought he would be.

"There is one more thing," Cortez said. "While the Agency wishes that you would have joined us, they're not an organization that can let you walk away."

The hairs on Floyd's arms stood up. He realized that Cortez had taken them downtown, where all the office buildings were. During the workday, the place was bustling with office workers. At night it was a ghost town, the high-rise buildings the only things to keep them company. Floyd glanced at the shadows around him.

"Are we really going to do this?" Floyd asked, raising his hands in defense.

Cortez didn't make a move. "I don't want to. I like you. All you have to do is come willingly."

"I already gave you my answer."

"I know. And I respect you for it."

No more than three seconds passed, but it seemed like eternity. Floyd turned and ran. Cortez said he had powers, but Floyd didn't know what they were. No point in finding out the hard way. He'd figure it out later.

Cortez didn't follow him. If Floyd could put some distance between them, he knew he could lose the smaller man.

Floyd's face slammed into something hard. He bounced off it and smacked into the ground. He got up, rubbing his hand to his sore face, warm blood crawling over his hand. He didn't see anything in front of him, just traffic in the distance and the warm glow of streetlights. Yet it felt as if he had run into a brick wall.

With a shaky hand, Floyd reached out in front of him. His fingers brushed up against...something. Floyd peered closer but couldn't see the transparent barrier. He changed directions and came up against it again, though not nearly as hard as the first time. Every turn he made he found himself boxed in. And Cortez stood calmly watching it all.

Cortez. *This was his power.*

The invisible box was shrinking. Floyd had to do something. He held his breath with each punch, striking the wall. With every blow the wall held firm. No matter his strength, the punches were getting him nowhere, and his cage shrunk smaller.

Floyd centered his mind as his enclosure shrunk. He held his breath and focused all his power into punching one spot. His hand broke free and Cortez grunted in pain. The rest of the invisible prison shattered. Floyd wasted no time in sprinting down the street, back to his familiar streets, leaving his pursuer behind.

CHAPTER 6

Floyd's head pounded as he ran. His vision blurred. His legs were sluggish and heavy. He must have hit that invisible wall harder than he thought. Cortez's footsteps echoed through the stone walls of the plaza. The empty streets between the slick, high-rise buildings made it impossible for Floyd to hide.

Just around the corner were stairs to the subway. Floyd hated to risk going down there. He might be able to lose Cortez in the throngs of people, but then innocent people could get in the way. And there was always the possibility of being trapped.

He didn't see any other way. Floyd ran to the subway entrance. Just as he passed the corner, he was snagged and pulled toward the wall. He sucked in his breath, raising his fist, ready to strike whoever had grabbed him.

"You," Floyd said. He released his breath and lowered his fist. It was the young kid from the corner store—the one with the with the old-school afro.

The teenager put a finger to his lips. Floyd pulled away but the teenager gripped him harder. Cortez was just about to round the corner. The teenager's wide eyes understood the danger that was about to come, but also warned Floyd not to run—not right now.

Floyd was tired of running, and he had questions. He decided to trust the kid. If it came to it, Floyd would fight Cortez. He nodded and stepped to the wall alongside the boy.

Cortez's footsteps stormed closer and closer. The kid held onto Floyd's arm but didn't wave or move. The sweat dripped down Floyd's temple and he gripped the kid's shoulder tight. The poor kid grunted and winced, and Floyd relaxed his grip.

Cortez stopped a mere six feet from them. His breathing echoed in Floyd's ear. "Damn it. Where did he go?" He swiveled his head and Floyd held his breath when his eyes glanced in their direction. It was over. Time to do it the hard way.

He began to move, but the kid pulled on Floyd, nearly toppling him over. Floyd almost yelled out, but Cortez started running toward the next street and disappeared from view.

The kid let go of Floyd and smiled.

Floyd stared at the kid. "What just happened?"

"We can't talk here. It's not safe. He may double back or there may be more on the way."

"I don't know even know your name. Why should I trust you?"

He gave a youthful smile. "My name is Noah. You can either trust me or take your chances with him. It's your choice."

Floyd thought about it. He could handle a kid much easier than Cortez. He nodded. "Name's Floyd."

"I know." Noah reached for Floyd's arm again. "Whatever you do, don't let go."

Floyd held onto his hand as they ran in the opposite direction of Cortez. As they crossed the invisible border of the polished, office buildings, the noise increased and more cars filled the roads. The buildings were older and dirtier. People walked about their business and Floyd had to watch where he stepped.

Noah let go of Floyd and a jogger almost ran into them.

"Hey, watch it!" the brightly dressed man yelled.

"Slow down," Noah said, putting his hands in his pockets. "Blend in."

Floyd breathed as they walked through the city. "Thanks, Noah. I take it you can turn invisible?"

He smiled. "How'd you guess?"

"Cortez looked straight at me and didn't see me." Floyd looked off in the distance and whistled. "You know when I was a kid, I wished I could have turned invisible."

Noah shrugged. "As my friend Mika would have said, 'invisible isn't the correct term.' The Agency calls it fading. People and technology can't see or track me."

"Wow," Floyd said. "That's quite a…trick." He wondered what other powers existed. But he had more important questions first.

"How do you know Cortez? Who does he work for?" Floyd asked.

"I don't know about any Cortez, but I know of the Agency. You're lucky he didn't have a Sentry with him. If he did, we wouldn't have been able to escape. It would have seen me and it's stronger than you." Noah hesitated. "They're dangerous. You should stay away from them."

"Why? What do they do?"

Noah shook his head. "They steal kids. They take them away from their families and force them to get in line and work for them." Silent tears fell down Noah's face and his voice was barely audible. "And they never get to see their families again."

Floyd clenched his fist and grit his teeth. He knew there was something Cortez had left out. Floyd needed to know more—he had to know what he was up against.

A loud bang distracted them. Floyd ducked and turned his head, seeing it was just two kids, kicking over a trash can.

"Hey, Noah—" But when Floyd turned back, Noah had gone.

Floyd had so many more questions, not only about Cortez's organization, but about Noah and where he came from. Floyd could clearly see that the kid needed help, but he wasn't the only one.

Floyd spent the night in the church's gym. The window still needed fixing. He was half tempted to fix it but there was an unwritten rule about that place. People snuck in there for hours or days at a time, but they respected it. No one threw parties, no tagging the walls, and no leaving trash anywhere. The church and the attached gym were both holy grounds. The preacher knew about it, and never said anything.

The next morning, Floyd headed for Juan's. He hated being out in the daylight, but it was easier to blend in with the thousands of people heading for work. Yet Floyd constantly looked over his shoulder, backtracked, and took the long way. For once, it wasn't the police he was worried about.

It was always risky going to people and places you knew and frequented. As soon as Floyd stepped into the building, he expected SWAT to rush him, or worse, Cortez. He allowed himself a moment of relief, then quickly made his way to Juan's apartment.

He still had his head on a swivel when he bowled over someone.

Floyd cursed when he saw who the old man was. "Mr. Patterson!"

"Jesus, Floyd. Watch where you're going. Why do you have to be so tall?"

"Sorry, sir. Let me help you up."

"Thank you." Mr. Patterson cleared his throat. "Now what in the blue blazes are you doing here?"

"Uhhh...I forgot my tools."

"I thought your aunt was ill," Mr. Patterson said, his beady eyes sharpening.

Floyd's eyes widened. He had forgotten about the lie he told Mr. Patterson.

"She is, sir," Floyd said. "But she still needs help around the house."

"Uh-huh."

Floyd knew Mr. Patterson wasn't buying it. The last thing Floyd needed was for him to call the cops. His face and video had been plastered all over the news. If there was one thing old people watched, it was cable news—whether or not what it told was the truth.

Mr. Patterson's eyes softened. "You take as much time as you need." He walked by and patted Floyd's arm. "I've always liked you, Floyd. You're a good man. Always trying to help people. Be safe."

As Floyd watched Mr. Patterson walk away, he realized there was more to the old man than he thought. More importantly, Floyd realized that he knew. *Had he always known?*

Floyd made his way toward Juan's apartment but thought of Shanice. He ached to see her one last time and feel her lips against his. He sighed. He couldn't risk it. Neither she nor her son deserved to have any heat on them.

When Floyd reached Juan's apartment, he pounded on the door. Juan yelled expletives from behind it, but Floyd kept on pounding.

Juan opened the door in anger. "What?" His eyes widened when he saw it was Floyd. "Amigo, it's you. I didn't think I'd see you again except in cuffs."

Floyd pushed aside his friend to quickly shut and lock the apartment door. "Thanks, man. You almost did. Sorry to do this to you, but I need your help."

Juan sighed. "I don't know. There's a lot of heat on you, like a ton."

Shit. Floyd had no idea what he would do if Juan wouldn't help. He didn't have any family nearby and no one else knew about his abilities. Not counting all the people who saw the videos of him.

"Don't be so serious, amigo." Juan smiled. "Relax. I got you."

Floyd returned the smile. "I owe you one."

"I know. What do you need? The cops can't do anything to you. From all the footage I've seen, they haven't ID'd you. They don't have a name and video is fuzzy. Good thing you all look alike. It'll blow over by the end of the week."

Juan might have been right. Then again, with all the bank robberies and the fact that he attacked cops, they might not let this one go so easily.

Floyd shook his head. "It's worse than that."

"What? Feds?"

"No."

Floyd quickly told Juan everything—about the organization, the strange kid helping him, how there are others with his abilities. It felt good to tell someone about all this craziness. Everyone else would have thought Floyd had gone insane. But Juan had been with him since the beginning.

"Dios mio," he said, putting his hand to his forehead. "You really stepped in it this time."

Floyd sighed. "I know. I need to get away from the city for a few days, maybe longer." He looked up and met Juan's gaze. "I'm thinking of using our rainy day money."

Juan's eyebrows raised and he looked away. After each job, they had stashed a small portion of the money away. It was only to be used for emergencies—if they needed a lawyer, a lifesaving procedure, or to bribe the right people. Floyd suspected Juan thought of it as a retirement fund. But that wasn't the purpose. The clouds had gathered and rain and lightning were coming.

Juan nodded, but seemed sad. "You do what you gotta do." Juan gave him a small smile. "That's what the money is there for, amiright?"

"Yeah."

"Let me get you a drink before you bounce. And you can tell me more about your crazy men-in-black stories."

Floyd sat on the couch while his friend went into the kitchen. He laid back and yawned, allowing himself to relax. This was the first time he had had a chance to be at ease. His body remembered countless times when they had hung out there, watching the game and drinking a beer.

I just need five minutes, Floyd told himself. *Just five minutes.* He shut his eyes, allowing sleep to claim him.

Floyd eyes fluttered open and he jolted.

"Jesus!" Juan said. "I hate when you do that. Can't you ever wake up like a normal person?"

Floyd peeled himself off the couch, feeling the aches and pains that accompany age, and yet the weariness of his body had disappeared. He glanced at the clock. He had slept for thirty minutes, but it seemed like an eternity.

He stretched his long arms and yawned. "I gotta go. Thanks for the break, Juan. I'll keep you posted."

"You sure you want to take off, man?"

Floyd nodded. "Yeah, I'm sure. Don't want you to get in trouble."

"What about the suits? You sure it's safe to go out there again? They found you once, they can find you again."

Floyd shrugged. "I have no choice."

"Stay a while, amigo. Where else you gonna go?"

Floyd stared at his friend. This wasn't like him. If the situation got too serious, Juan would rather bail than stick around. "Juan, what—"

"Hold up." His phone beeped and he checked his phone. "I gotta take this."

Floyd watched him move into the kitchen and his annoyance rose. *What could Juan possibly gain from this? He wouldn't go to the cops or the Feds.* Whoever was on the phone couldn't be more important than what was going on right now.

When Juan came back into the room, Floyd saw that he was wrong.

"Cortez."

Right behind Cortez was another man. His slim, tall body moved oddly. He had lifeless eyes that stared directly at Floyd. The pale man's gaze never wavered from Floyd, and his blinks were long and steady.

"Good to see you again, Floyd," Cortez said. "I'm not mad. I'm impressed. I won't be the only one."

Floyd took a step back. "Even though I got away from you."

Cortez chuckled. "Yes. They'll be impressed with the way you use your powers. A tip: that's the way to get to them. Impress them with your gifts and you'll go far."

"But only if I work for them."

"Of course. We can't have you robbing any more banks."

Floyd appeared to consider his offer, but was only thinking of his friend. "Leave Juan alone and I'll go with you willingly."

Cortez looked to Juan, then bent over and laughed. His companion remained silent.

"Who do you think called me?" Cortez said.

Floyd glared at his longtime friend. He almost said that he didn't think that it would be possible, that he would never believe Juan would betray him. But Floyd knew better. For as long as Floyd knew Juan, he was always about the money. Juan knew better than to openly flaunt it, but it didn't mean he didn't indulge.

Floyd had no words, but anger flooded his eyes.

"Uh, I better go," Juan said.

Juan grabbed his coat and scurried out of his own apartment.

Cortez snorted. "Didn't even say goodbye. Suppose it's for the best. Floyd, I like you, I really do. So I'm giving you one last chance to come along with me peacefully."

"Or what?"

"Or my friend here will make you."

Floyd shifted his body toward the silent man next to Cortez. He just stared blankly at Floyd, his gaze forever unflinching.

Cortez sighed and pinched his nose's bridge. "Take care of him."

The Silent Man methodically stepped closer. After experiencing what Cortez could do, Floyd was more worried about him. But the agent seemed content to let his partner capture Floyd. The man made no move to defend himself. Floyd held his breath and threw a strong left jab. It felt like hitting a steel wall. Floyd held his breath again, this time cocking his right arm and putting all his weight into the punch before swinging at the man's head.

The man's neck snapped back, hanging at an awkward angle.

Shit. Floyd didn't mean to kill the guy.

The man grabbed his head and straightened it back into place. "Designation: Floyd Taylor. Ability: super strength by way of holding in air."

Floyd took a step back. *This must be one of those sentries Noah talked about. But how do I—"*

The sentry moved fast, dealing a blow to Floyd's stomach, forcing Floyd to crumple to the ground. "Solution: take away target's ability to breathe."

Cortez knelt over Floyd. "I warned you."

Jesus, Floyd thought. He had never been hit that hard before. *What are these things made of?*

The pain flooding his body was easing. All Floyd had to do was—

The sentry struck him again. Floyd puked, spilling his lunch over Juan's floor.

"Those things pack quite a punch," Cortez said. "If only you had done this the easy way. Take him. I haven't got all day."

The sentry raised his fist only to stop. It twisted toward Cortez. "Query: another Singularity is in the vicinity."

Cortez turned his head. "What are you—"

Floyd caught a glimpse of something that looked like a flare. Before he could cover his head, it exploded in the room. A blinding light seared his eyes and a sonic sound pierced his ears. Small arms pulled him away and he let himself be guided, nearly tripping on his own two feet. He followed blindly, then felt the cool night air brush his cheeks and the stench of too many people flood his nose.

"Come on," a familiar voice said.

"Noah? That you?"

"Yeah, we haven't much time, and you're heavy. Can you make it?"

Floyd rubbed his eyes and nodded. The stars still shone in his eyes, but he and Juan had been

down that emergency exterior stairwell countless times in their youth.

Bells rang in Floyd's ears, and his body swayed like he had spent all day climbing the stairs of a ten-story building when the elevators were out. But he made it down with Noah's help. Floyd leaned against the alley wall.

Glass shattered above, raining down on Floyd.

"Move!" Noah shouted. "It's the sentry."

The sentry's steps thundered as it descended the stairs. Noah pulled him out of the alley and into the streets.

While the blinding morning sun hurt Floyd's eyes. It was early—way too early. Bright enough to be tracked and followed. The crowd of people going to work had started to thin.

The pair reached the intersection and the light had turned red. Floyd wanted to go but Noah grabbed his arm, holding him back.

"Why don't you just make us disappear?" Floyd asked as they waited for the crosswalk light to change.

"Uh-uh." Noah shook his head. "It doesn't work like that, not with the sentries. Using our powers is like a beacon to them if they're close by. That's what they were originally designed for. They already know what we look like, but it'll take time for them to scan and recognize us."

The light changed and the pair began walking. Floyd looked back to see if the sentry was following them.

"Don't!" Noah said. "All it takes is a second for them to see your face. Stay cool."

"How do you know so much about them?"

Noah hesitated. "I can take you to a place. You'll learn as much as I know. Do you want to come?"

Floyd paused. A man bumped into him, but Floyd didn't care. Floyd had no idea of what to expect from the world he had stepped into. Both Noah and Cortez offered him a choice to learn more. Even though Floyd needed answers, he had no reason to trust any of them. But as Floyd stared at Noah's young face and eyes, he was reminded of himself in simpler times. *Especially with that afro.*

"OK, Noah. I'll go with you."

"Great," he said, and smiled.

"There's just something I gotta do first."

Floyd knew he should go with Noah. Learning more was the smart play. But Floyd also knew that he couldn't let Juan get away, not after what he did. He knew Juan would make a play for the money soon.

Noah nodded. "I get it." He turned to head in the other direction.

Floyd grabbed his arm. "How can I get in touch with you?"

Noah pulled his arm back. "Don't worry. I'll be around." Then he faded from Floyd's eyes.

I don't think I'll ever get used to that. Floyd took off down the street, both fearful and anxious of what he might learn.

CHAPTER 7

Early in their bank robbing career, Floyd and Juan set up an emergency fund to save a portion of each job. Against Juan's objections, they stashed more money than Juan thought they should. Neither of them ever expected anything to go smoothly. They always thought it'd be used for a lawyer or for a getaway. But how to keep that much cash close by without getting robbed themselves?

There was a portion of the city gentrification hadn't touched yet. All major cities had spots like this, but there was one street almost beyond the city limits with a house some said was haunted. It had been abandoned and boarded up years ago after a man had killed his wife, his children, and then himself there. Even with all the homelessness in the city, no one spent the night in it.

Floyd shivered, staring at the old house. The steel gate hung off its hinges in welcome. Even with his power, he felt nervous about going inside. His Gammy always said people stayed away from places like this due to bad spirits. He couldn't listen to her advice now.

He pulled out a small flashlight and squeezed through the open front door. The shadows stared at him, their faces moving with each step he took. The hairs on his arms stood up. *It's just an old house.* But after seeing the things he had recently, maybe his Gammy had a point.

A scurrying sound rattled his ears. Floyd sucked in his breath and spun around. A rat as large as his foot ran along the baseboards.

He exhaled. "Rats. I hate rats." Only they would dare venture into the murder house.

Floyd slowly made his way through the abandoned house, trying to avoid more furry friends. He had only been inside the house once, but Juan had hidden their stash in the master bedroom in the farthest corner of the top floor.

Both the chalk outlines and stained blood had faded over the years, but Floyd still cringed at the evidence of what had happened here. His own dad had been violent at times. Thankfully, he left before things reached these depths.

When Floyd reached the master bedroom, he glanced around, looking for Juan or any signs that he had already taken the money. After all, Cortez had given Juan a head start. Floyd bent down and smashed the floorboard. He wanted Juan to know he had been there.

Floyd exhaled. The duffel bag was still there, and so was the money. *Good. Juan doesn't deserve it after betraying me.* At least that was one thing Floyd didn't have to worry about. Still, denying Juan the money wasn't as fulfilling as he thought. His former friend deserved more punishment than this. If only Floyd could see the look on Juan's face when he discovered the money was missing.

"You're getting predictable, amigo."

The closet door opened, and out came Juan.

Floyd stood. "You're not getting this money."

"Sure I am. But that money is chump change. I've got an opportunity here, and you are going to help."

"The hell I will," Floyd said. He took a step forward, but hesitated. Juan wouldn't have come here unprepared.

"Cortez didn't believe me. He didn't think you'd come back here. What's money to you when you can easily get money with your powers?" Juan paused. "But I knew better." His eyes narrowed and his nostrils flared. "I knew you'd have to play the hero and stop me, the bad guy, from getting what's mine. Just like you have since we were kids."

Floyd caught his breath. *Is that what he thinks of me?* Gammy's words echoed in his head. *There are those who are going to want what you have.*

Floyd took a step forward. "If you knew that, then why did you come alone?"

"I didn't."

The closet burst off its hinges and someone appeared beside Juan. It's dead and lifeless stare fixated on Floyd. Floyd's breath caught in his throat—the Sentry.

"He gave you one of those machines?" Floyd asked. "They have to be worth a fortune. Surprised he didn't think you'd run off with it."

Juan shrugged. "Wish I could. But who would I sell it to? It was hard to convince Cortez to let me borrow it. Besides, it doesn't take orders from me. I'm merely assisting it in capturing you. Once I do, then I'll have my way in with the Agency. It's a test. One I'm going to pass."

The sentry approached Floyd. Juan leaned back against the wall and crossed his arms. "I know you're not going to make this easy."

Floyd closed his fists and readied himself. He wished the kid had been able to tell him more about them. Especially what their weaknesses were. Floyd sucked in his breath and struck the machine with light and rapid punches. The sentry didn't register the weak attacks. It reached out with its arms and Floyd ducked under them.

OK. Need to try something harder.

Floyd cocked his arm back and aimed for the sentry's head, mustering as much force as he had in Juan's apartment.

The sentry caught it.

"Subject's attacks analyzed. Response initiated."

With its free hand, the sentry struck Floyd in his throat. Even though Floyd had held his breath, increasing his strength, he still felt the machine's force. He gagged, gasping for air. The machine struck again. Floyd collapsed to his knees.

"Jesus…" He gasped. *It's stronger than last time.* For all his power and strength, he had forgotten what it felt like to be hit like that. Floyd couldn't help but hear his dad's voice: "There's always someone stronger."

Floyd pushed himself off the ground, wiping blood from his mouth. This wasn't over yet.

"Christ, amigo. Stay down," Juan said. "From what Cortez told me, you're no match for one of these things on your best day. I don't want to see you get hurt."

Doesn't he? That didn't matter. All that mattered was stopping Juan. If Floyd had to go through a sentry then so be it.

Floyd gathered his strength and centered himself. *It's a machine.* Which meant Floyd had to release the restraints he normally placed on himself. He didn't have to hold back.

"Come on!" Floyd roared and lunged at the machine. He grabbed its arms until they started to crack. Floyd swung like an Olympian hammer thrower, smashing the sentry into the wall on the opposite side. He picked up a piece of the broken headboard and flung it at the sentry like a spear. Sparks sizzled and dark liquid leaked from its chest as his aim rung true.

The machine rose. "Sufficient damage sustained. Increasing threat level to appropriate response."

The sentry's eyes glowed red. A beam of light flew at Floyd. Floyd moved but it struck his shoulder, and he yelped.

Even though Floyd had held his breath, the light had burned his upper right shoulder and incinerated part of his shirt. What would have happened if he hadn't been using his powers? What other abilities did the sentry have?

"Did you see that?" Juan said, laughing. "Laser beams from his eyes. Didn't see that coming! It's like a dog! What other tricks can it do?"

Yeah, a dog that can take my hand off. And the rest of me.

Juan sighed. "Cortez needs you alive. You're going to him no matter what. Might as well make it in one piece. You can't beat this machine alone."

Floyd stood up and glanced around, looking for anything he might use as shield or a weapon.

The sentry's eyes lit up but then stopped. It cocked its head. "Danger. Multiple singularities incoming. Initiate defenses."

Noah shimmied into view behind Floyd. And he wasn't alone. Four other teenagers surrounded the short kid. "Destroy it," he said.

The teenagers yelled and let go of Noah, heading for the sentry.

"Wait!" Floyd reached out with his arm, but grunted in pain.

"It's all good," Noah said, rushing over to him, helping Floyd stand.

Floyd watched as one teenager flipped off the floor, her feet landing on the ceiling and staying there. Her hair hung down as she ran toward the sentry. Another kid grew bone-like spikes from his arms and tossed one to the girl. She yelled and threw it at the sentry, spearing it. Floyd's mouth was agape as he watched the teenagers tear the sentry apart.

"How can you destroy it so easily?" Floyd asked.

"We've had lots of practice." Noah's face hardened. "And we're lucky. There's only one, and an agent isn't around." He stared at Floyd. "We make it a point to not fight these things one-on-one and to destroy them as quickly as possible. If you let it adapt and learn, it *will* beat and kill you."

The girl walked back across the ceiling with the sentry's head dangling from her hands. "I wish we could take these. They'd make for great trophies."

"You know we can't, Kara."

She shrugged then tossed the head. "A girl can dream." She glared at Juan. "What should we do with him? I can't collect sentry heads but human heads will do just fine."

Juan's head spun as he tried to look for a way out. He put his sweaty hands up, backing toward the cracked window as the teenagers approached him.

"Wait," Floyd said.

Juan sighed and slumped over. "Thanks, amigo."

"Don't thank me yet. What were you planning to do with me?"

"Yo man, like I said. I didn't want to see you get hurt." He paused.

"But?"

"I was just going to turn you over to Cortez. He said you wouldn't get hurt. It's just that they had a place for people like you."

Floyd rubbed his hands across his bald head. "All this for a job? So you can go legit?"

"Oh no, you got it wrong. Look around you, man. The people Cortez works for have access to all kinds of shit. And they pay well."

"Money?" Kara screamed. "You want to torture us for money!" She grabbed a bone spear from what was left of the sentry's body and stalked toward him.

Noah grabbed her. "Wait. It's not our call. It's his."

Floyd stared at Noah and his friends. *Their eyes.* They seemed much, much older than their years suggested. What things had they seen? What had been done to them? But those were questions for later.

As Floyd stared at Juan, he couldn't help but wonder what had happened to his old friend. Had he always been like this and Floyd just not realized?

"Let him go," Floyd said.

"Go?" Kara said. "Go? You may let him go. We don't have to. You're not one of us. You don't know what they did to us."

"Listen to him," Noah said. Despite being smaller and younger than her, none of the other teenagers argued.

Juan scooted around the teenagers, moving to the door as quickly as he could.

"Juan," Floyd said.

His old friend stopped and raised his head.

"Don't ever let me see you again."

A sly smile spread across Juan's face. He snorted before running out the door.

"I can't believe you let him go," Kara said, her hands clenched. "You don't know what they do to people like us!"

"Then tell me."

"What?"

"Tell me what I don't know," Floyd said.

Noah looked to the others then scrunched his face. He looked back at Floyd. "You know. That's not a bad idea."

"Noah—" Kara said.

"He's one of us."

"But he's not from there!"

"And he's old," the boy with the bone spears said. The teenagers all snickered.

"You're both right," Noah said. He shrugged. "We'll let her decide."

Floyd raised his eyebrows, but stayed quiet. He stuffed the money into the duffel bag and slung it over his shoulder. Noah and the other kids led Floyd away from the house while Noah told their story.

The Agency had a school that they all had been in. The school tortured the kids, testing their powers and pushing their limits. Thanks to Noah, most of them had been able to escape.

So that's why they look up to Noah, even though he's half their height.

They went into the subway, past the platforms into the tunnels that only trains dared venture into. The darkened tunnels split off until they were abandoned by technology and commuters. The only things there were rats and people looking for a place to hide from the cold nights outside.

The dead, stale air made Floyd's nose and skin itch. The sea of people parted for their little group. They ventured deeper into the tunnels with only the rats and sounds of dripping water keeping them company.

They reached a tunnel sealed by old boards. They pricd off a few, more than usual, Floyd thought, based on how hard it was to pull out the nails on the higher boards, but finally made a hole big enough for him to fit through, and they all stepped inside. Dim lights shone in the darkness, strung like Christmas lights above his head. A couple dozen more teenagers milled around. All conversations stopped as heads swiveled to Floyd.

"Didn't realize we were having company." The teenagers parted and a lithe middle-aged woman with long blond hair appeared. She sighed and brought her fingers to the bridge of her nose. "Noah, I thought we discussed this."

He couldn't meet her eyes. "Sorry. Things changed."

Kara came forward. "I told him, we shouldn't bring him here. I said—"

With a glare, the woman silenced her.

The smaller woman stepped to Floyd, her fierce blue eyes meeting his. "We have a lot to discuss, Mr..."

"Floyd."

She gave a tight-lipped smile. "Mia."

She took him through the train tunnels. Old appliances were piled in one corner. A chubby boy smacked and yelled at an oven. Lights flickered throughout the place. Most of the rooms were dark or had uneven candles lighting them. They passed one room whose smell crept into Floyd's throat, nearly causing him to gag.

Mia's room was well away from the bad smells and kids yelling. Yet Floyd knew she would be there in an instant if anything went wrong. Her room was small and she lit a candle next to her tiny bed. She overturned a large bucket and indicated for Floyd to sit on it. "Sorry. I don't receive many guests down here."

"I can see that."

They sat in silence for several moments.

Finally, Mia said, "You trouble me, Floyd."

He raised his eyebrows. "Oh. How so?"

"You're an unknown factor with the strength of a sentry."

"Worried I'll hurt you?"

She smirked. "God, no. I'm worried about the kids."

Floyd stared back the way they came. "That's quite an army you're raising here."

Mia leaned forward. "Is that what you think?"

Floyd thought about Noah and the others experiences. "What else could it be?"

"We're at war. The Agency has done things to all of us, and it's time for a reckoning." She turned her head to wipe away tears.

"People always use kids in their wars."

Her head snapped up, and her eyes were ablaze with anger. "There's a lot you don't know."

"I know enough. And I don't like you using kids in your personal war."

The anger in her eyes burned even brighter. Floyd worried he might have pushed her too far. He also realized that she may have had powers herself. He sucked in his breath.

Mia let out a breath of air and her shoulders relaxed. "Then stay here and join us. It'd be nice to have another adult in the room." She gave a small smile and he released his breath.

Floyd shook his head. "No. I don't want to be a part of your war."

"They'll never leave you alone. Not now. Trust me on that. But all right. Have one of the kids show you the way out."

Floyd rose. He stopped at the doorway and almost apologized for what had happened to them. Instead, the sound of dripping water rung in his head. It reminded him of all those pipes and faucets he fixed during simpler times.

Floyd took a step from the corner of his eye and a familiar afro shimmered away. He really did remind Floyd of his nephew. This time, Floyd vowed to not make the same mistake. He could be there. Be here.

"You know," he said, "you need someone to fix all the things around here." He raised his eyebrows and smirked. "I may know a guy."

Mia stood up and placed her hand on his shoulder. Her watery eyes stared at him. "Thank you. This place could use some fixing up."

He took her hand in his.

Floyd knew he couldn't go back to his old life. More importantly, someone had to be there for the kids.

CHAPTER 8

Cortez stood in what was left of the abandoned house. The cleaning crews were already cataloging and filing what they could. Normally, they'd have to repair and restore, but the abandoned house was already almost destroyed. No loss there. Should have been demolished years ago.

He stared at the head of the Sentry. After letting Floyd get away the first time, he had finally been authorized to use one of these in the field. Now it was in pieces. His bosses weren't going to like that at all. If only he had known there would be more than one or two singularities, he could have gotten authorized for two, or at least a weapon.

He kicked the sentry's head, watching it bounce to the other side of the room. Juan's gaze was on Cortez's back. Cortez turned to look at him and the nervous man quickly looked away, stuffing his hands into his pockets.

"That's no way to treat our property," a woman said.

Cortez turned and stood face to face with the boss of all bosses—Zelda.

The small, old woman had hawkish features with a stare to match. Nothing got past her. From what he had heard, she had been with the Agency from the beginning, building it to what it was now.

"Sorry, ma'am," Cortez said. "Just frustrated. A Singularity got away."

"More than one." She didn't seem surprised. She never was. "I'm more concerned with why you thought it best to work with a civilian even after you were authorized for a sentry. You couldn't handle this on your own?"

"No, ma'am. Uh, I mean yes, ma'am. I could handle it, but he knew the target. He informed me that the target would be here. I thought he would have gone back to that woman of his." Cortez hesitated.

He thought of lying, but that wouldn't get him any-where. "I was trying to cover more ground."

From the corner of her eye, Zelda stared at Juan. Juan slunk away and went outside.

"No matter," Zelda said. "You had no idea what you were up against."

"Floyd? I could have handled him even without the sentry. I wasn't expecting the kids though, and I wasn't here. We could have taken them. It would have been easier if I had a standard firearm."

Zelda walked toward the window and stared out. "No. You couldn't handle Amelia."

"Christ," Cortez said, putting a hand to his sweaty forehead. He had heard the stories of the most infa-mous Singularity in the Agency, and what had hap-pened between her and Zelda. How does one stop a ghost?

"You shouldn't have given the civilian the use of the Sentry."

"It wouldn't have done what he said. It only—"

Zelda turned to look at him, and Cortez shut up.

She stood with her hands behind her back, looking at...everything and nothing as far as Cortez could tell.

"Can this man be an asset?" Zelda asked.

"I believe so. He knows his friend and is eager to apprehend him." Cortez fidgeted. "It'll take time."

"Make it happen then. Give him limited access and resources—enough to track his friend."

"He'll expect a reward."

"Good. Money makes a man easier to control when it's all they care about." She turned and stared out the cracked window again. "Amelia is planning something. It's only a matter of time before she makes her move. We must be ready."

AUTHOR'S CORNER

Email: marcjohnson@marcanthonyjohnson.com

Facebook: http://www.facebook.com/MarcJohnsonAuthor

Goodreads: http://www.goodreads.com/marcjohnson

Newsletter: https://rb.gy/6ru8lc

Twitter: http://www.twitter.com/Hellsfire

Website: http://www.marcanthonyjohnson.com